UNFORGIVEN

BY THERESE

ISBN: 978-0-909497-77-4

Illustrations: Constance Hunter
conhunterart@gmail.com

Design & Artwork:
Purple Possum Design
purplepossumdesign.com.au

*This story is written with thanks
to those who stare down the truth every day,
and as apology to those who deserved so much more.*

THE MAN'S STORY

Even the moon hid her light
from the eyes of mortals
on the night I was born.
A wintry wind howled among the hills,
while rain pounded on the roof
like demonic vagrants demanding entry.
On such a dismal night,
I made my arrival into this world
that would never befriend me.

Born on a night
that lay between the signs,
between the crab and the lion,
and, throughout
my pitiful existence,
it has become clear
that neither sun-sign
wished to house me.

Yet I chose to be known
as one born to the house of Leo.
I fancied the roaring lion
more than the scurrying crab.

An unwanted child was I,
an increase in the burden
already resting uneasily
upon the shoulders
of an unhappy union.

Secondborn was I, following the girl,
the stronger following the weak
and, throughout our lives,
she would follow me instead,
creep along in my shadow,
until I ceased to see her.

Even so, we held to each other.
As possessions, pawns,
tokens to be won in the games
that commenced, won by each side
and then put away in a box.

No mercy from ungrateful parents
No mercy from unfriendly elementals
No mercy from the frosty stars
that drew the map
of my destiny.
For my birth,
I am unforgiven.

My mind was fast,
in motion, a wonder to behold.
Even as a child, innocent
as they say all children must be,
I learned the sin of pride
and its stain upon my soul
was indelible.

Sharing a classroom,
the younger child,
placed before the first,
by my presence
belittling my sister.

As teachers paraded me,
other children despised me,
my sister, my own sister,
sought to ridicule.
For my intelligence,
a sparkling jewel
cut poorly
by unskilled hands
and set in rusting iron,

I am unforgiven.

*B*ored,
contemptuous of a society
beneath my worth,
a lion-cub breathing disdain
upon all who dared walk,
without consent,
upon the hills and plains
of my kingdom.

I learnt quickly
to play the games
of an adult world,
a leonine cub batting at fragile minds,
like playing with my food.
Adult and child,
rich and poor,
male, female,
sincere or dishonest,
it made no difference.

All that mattered
was that I took my dues
from loyal subjects
As a dauphin, a king in waiting.

For this,
I am unforgiven.
As are they.

A family divided,
violently torn apart
with wild anger,
betrayal,
recriminations.

My sister and I became
the coveted trophies,
Brought out of the cupboard
in full display, testimony
to the greater strength,
the greater power
of, alternately,
mother, then father,
then mother,
then father,
and all the while
they played so with us,
we fed upon their anger
so it became a monster, a charybdis,
its wild, swirling whirlpool
sucking us all down, broken ships,
into its greedy belly, until
we were all lost.

But, the saving Official Graces
refereeing the games
and, at intervals, removing
us, the children, the prize
from the playing field,
sending us
to compassionate families
where the games
were played with greater subtlety
and we learnt the codes,
the Darwinian codes,
survival of the fittest.

In the savage storms,
firm against the winds,
stood an old man,
the grandfather.
Into his welcoming arms I fled,
to his sanctuary where a lion-cub
could create his own kingdom
to replace that of his heritage,
which had been razed to the ground.

In came the officials,
with note-pad and pen
and judge's gavel.
They didn't like
the grandfather's magic wand
and the way he waved it,
though it gave me no grief
carving, as it did, a spell
of affection and need.

But such was not permitted
for one like I,
"This child
may not smile,
he is of the unforgiven."

From parent to parent,
government-approved family,
to another,
to another,
to another,
fleeing to my grandfather's arms,
and begin the round again.

My childhood,
learning the survival skills
and the forbidden excitements
taught by the gypsy children,
slight of hand, flick of finger,
charm with a smile, turn of a heel,
how to hide in light and shade,
spin the fortunes, then disappear.
Once learned, become the teacher,
Surpassing all.

Such a life!
Such an exhilarating,
dangerous existence!
Such an adventure!
I grew to love
the intricacies of the game.
I became a master,
playing with them all,
and always, always
one move ahead.

For this, I am unforgiven.

*A*dults
are never as free
as children,
even children
such as I.
Many tried
to claim my soul,
but a soul divided amongst so many
accords only the smallest portion
to each claimant,
only the hint
of the fey will o' the wisp.

As I grew,
and I grew tall,
pretending to a more mature age,
laughing at the ease of deception,
the shadow of a cross
darkened my path,
voices calling for me to take it up,
carry it for them, because
they were too weak, needed
me to bear their burdens.

Not for me, the climb to Calvary
with its painful redemption.
I grasped eagerly
when the chance of escape arrived.

In the distance,
I saw a new world
of uneducated, untamed savages
who would not doubt
their inferiority
as soon as they saw
the whiteness of my skin
and the golden cross
I wore upon my collar.

In the distance,
I saw the highlands
of a rich and abundant,
an unexplored land where,
finally, I could carve my kingdom.

As I claimed my kingdom,
my kingdom claimed me.
In that place,
I came as close
as ever I came
in this pitiful existence,
to a stillness of mind
and a peace of spirit.

Unearned!
I entered paradise
illegitimately,
it is only allowed
to those prepared
to walk the road to Golgotha.

For this, I am unforgiven.

I **knew this,** as I read from the gospels
to my illiterate disciples, knew
the story meant for me.

>The man they called Jesus
>hung wearily upon the cross
>he had accepted,
>though an innocent man,
>because he loved
>and took into his heart
>the burdens of others,
>calling them his own.
>
>Beside him hung another,
>weighed down
>with the shame of sinning.
>"Jesus," he asked,
>"Can you forgive me?"
>
>The sinner asked so
>because he knew
>that Jesus carried
>the burden of all hurts,
>of all wrongs.

Though all light
had drained from the world,
the truth still shone.

To the sinner
who had accepted
his self-made cross,
the sinner
who now sought forgiveness,
Jesus promised
that there was a place
in the Kingdom
for him.

But for the third man,
who hung beside them,
one who mocked rather than pleaded,
he remained, eternally,
the Unforgiven.

That man was me.

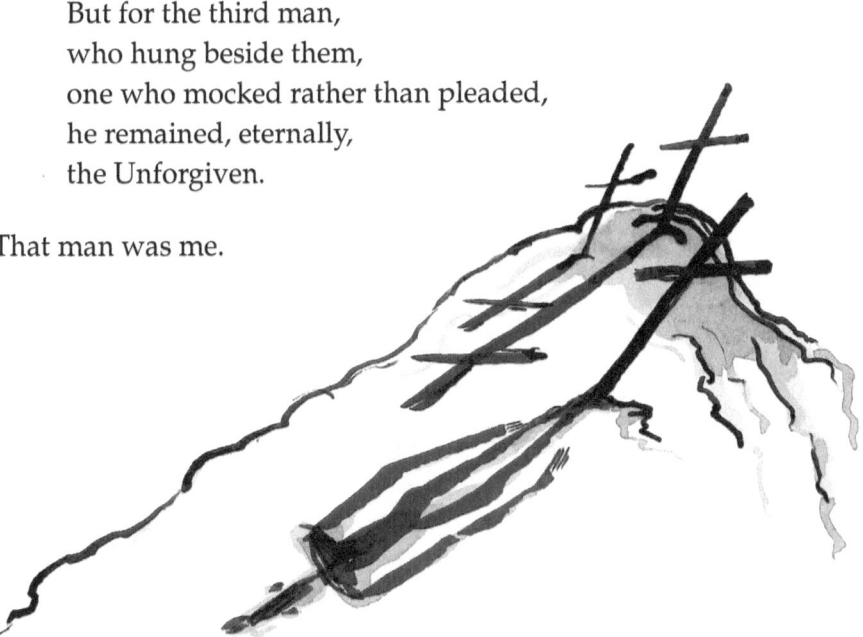

"**Y**our country calls!
March proudly, our son,
as you carry
your weapons of war.
March proudly,
and never forget,
not even for a moment
that as you thrust
your shiny, steel bayonet
into the gut
of the enemy,
that you do so
to make this world
a better place,
a freer place,
a happier place."

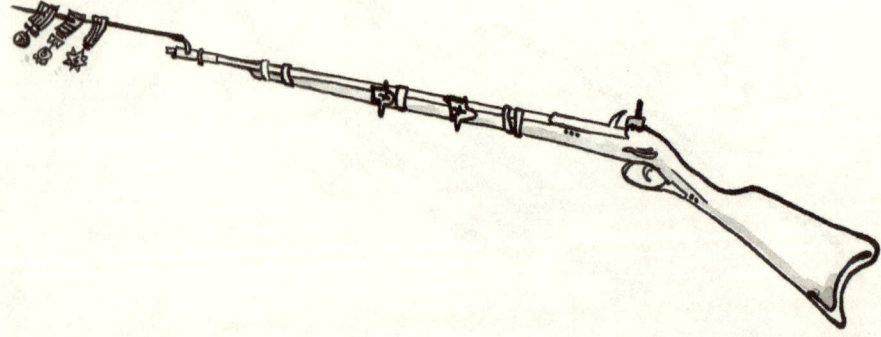

So I left the highlands,
a king departing
upon the crusades,
never doubting
that I would return
adorned with
the medals of valour,
of honour,
of a hero.
I forgot about the scars,
and for that,
I am unforgiven.

*O*f course,
they recognised
the superiority
of my mind.
Though I laughed in their faces,
I gained the respect
of the other soldiers
when I refused
the officer's garb
and chose instead
to march beside
the ordinary man.

Returning to games familiar,
exhilarating,
but so familiar.
I knew well enough
how un-ordinary I was.

Still,
when they'd told us
to take pride
in the enemy's slaughter,
they forgot to mention
that sometimes the enemy would come
in the guise of children
and, at first, my stomach rebelled
when I looked into
the boy's wide and slanted eyes
and, seeing my reflection there,
knew that I would be destroying
my own self, and that
I could not do.

There were new rules
to this game,
to the games of war,
but I learnt quickly
and locked away
that part of self,
learned
not to look into the eyes
of this strange,
chameleonic,
deadly enemy.

Remember the medals
to be worn proudly
upon the breast
in the victory parade
that would welcome
a king's homecoming.

For this, I am unforgiven.

The rules
were not so different
to those I had learned
at an earlier age.

Once again,
the student
became the teacher,
only, the leader of men,
not gypsy boys, and
the price of a wrong move
was higher,
not just their lives
but my own,
and upon the latter
I placed great value.

The men I led,
they accorded me
great respect,
paid the dues
I had always known
to be mine,
and I treated my minions
with care and concern,
taking pride
in the administration
of my responsibility.
The stain of the sin
set deeper and darker.

Between the fighting,
such fun we had!
My soldiers and I
had nought but each other.
To stave off loneliness
and a longing
for the paddocks of home,
with the fresh odour
of sunburned lands
smelling sweet
in our memories,
surrounded as we were
by the stench of blood
and rotting vegetation,
I set their minds
to games
that grew ever more amusing.

Games against the bureaucracy,
Games against the coward,
Games against the gullible yanks.
We laughed,
we played like children,
deaf to the relentless screams
that echoed down through the hills,
and ever, ever, in the caverns
of our minds.

For this, I am unforgiven.

Some have called me cocky,
arrogant,
but I always took due care,
and it was
through no such fault
that, as my men followed,
we walked into
the dragon's lair,
into
his waiting maws.

Through the years,
the aeons that followed,
I came to know
the enemy
as never before,
and I feared
that I had finally, mistakenly,
found my way
up that hill to Calvary,
hanging now upon a cross
while the vultures circled,
awaiting the feast.

As I looked around
and each day saw
my men, my faithful soldiers,
hanging in bamboo cages
under a searing sun,
with fingernails pulled
and flesh sliced away,
or set, one against the other,
for our captor's amusement,
as I watched
my own body
beaten and torn,
and endured
the 'attitude adjustments'
stimulated
by the electric shocks,
I came to understand
human cruelty
in a totally new way.

Always, always,
I avoided the final death
and I found
the way of escape,
taking with me
the few who remained,
for if I relinquished
the proud self,
I relinquished all.

Some things cannot
be escaped, and
that place
remains with me still,
with all the images
of cruelty.

For this, I am unforgiven.

Where,
the hero's welcome,
the waving banners
and sounding trumpets
to celebrate
the king's victorious return?

Where,
the subjects
waiting eagerly
for the stories gathered
that would make them laugh,
make them cry,
make them applaud?

Greeted instead
with rotten tomatoes
that again stained
the fresh-pressed uniforms
with the colour of blood.

Greeted instead
with angry accusations
from the ones
who did not accept
the very human need,
the need of every male
to earn the badge
of his manhood
in the blood rites.

Greeted instead
by ignorant innocents
who cried out
"Murderers, you are unforgiven!"

*I*rrepressible intelligence!
Weary though my body was,
I knew still
that someday
they would recognise
my right to the throne!

The same games,
only the pieces
varied in design.
Once carved from driftwood,
then from cold, hard steel,
now from timeless oak.

I took a bride,
quickly, for I wished
to reinstate myself,
and I sired my children.

Once again, the patterns of the past
repeating, endlessly repeating...
the elder girl,
and the second-born son.
A chance, for them,
to be the recipients
of all I had learned,
the chance, for them,
to change the patterns of heritage,
the chance, through them,
to make the world
as it should have been for me,
through them,
the new generation of royalty.

I became the king,
small-town though it was
and my children
did reap the benefits
of my exalted existence.
Finally, it had come to me,
the Midas touch
that so many think
is only found
in children's tales.

I built bridges and castles and roads,
strong monuments to my talent.
I built care and concern
amongst that small-minded community
and their gratitude was balm
to this frustrated regent,
was further food
for the stain of pride
that spread across my soul.
I wondered
if I might find mercy
in such a place,
afraid of the day
they would discover
how often had fallen
my thrones.

I did not dare tell them,
untrusting of their mercy,
for which omission,
I am unforgiven.

I had chosen my queen unwisely.
She grew discontented,
despising the gifts
I lavished upon her,
despising my status,
ridiculing my manhood.

She took other lovers,
taunting me with their youth
and the vigour
of their untested bodies.

Like the dark hag,
she plotted for my downfall,
jealous of my throne.
It is not good
when a king
is so publicly scorned
by his own, chosen queen.

In the dark of the night
she set the rot
into the bulwarks
and foundations,
even as the semen
of another
trickled down her thighs.

But it was
in the light of day
that she left with her lover,
one with whom
I had once shared friendship,
and she took my children,
my hope of redemption,
with her.

For a time,
only for a time,
the lion wearied,
hiding in his cave
and licking his wounds,
trying to escape
the nightmares
of a scuttling crab
as it burrowed
deep into the sand.

When he emerged,
his kingdom
had been given
to another, and
those who had been subject
turned their faces away.
Their king,
their brave, bold, oh so strong king,
had failed them,
and was unforgiven.

The oaken pieces,
warped and twisted
from too much exposure
to stormy weather,
were discarded.

In a place of learning
I found a new set,
moulded with care,
painted in hues
of purple and green,
smooth to the touch.

I delighted in the learning,
for it released
the essence of roses
into my mind
and I discovered
something new in the playing,
I discovered the feminine,
a world where others
truly cared,
truly shared,
and offered their homes
to those who had none,
offered their homes
to the gypsy children.

I knew those children!

It seemed that
the long road
had indeed returned me
to the place of my beginnings,
to learn again and, maybe,
this time, get it right.

I was welcomed,
welcomed by the children,
welcomed as a hero returned,
welcomed as a man of worldly wisdom,
welcomed as a knight
whose scars shone
like medals well-earned.

It was in this place
that I found a princess
whose heart was pure,
and tried and strong.
Slowly, carefully,
I unfolded my life
in offering to her,
and won the greatest prize,
a woman's love.
She told me I was forgiven.

THE WOMAN'S STORY

Of roses and the ballet,
that was how he saw me then,
of hope and angelic countenance.
I believed his word,
believed that he saw me so,
for who wishes to doubt such praise!

Of strength and love and integrity,
that was how I saw him,
of shining soul,
with the dross seared away
by the fires of his life.
I saw his love
for the gypsy children,
his gentleness and care.
They were the same children
whom I had long
taken into my heart,
and I rejoiced
to see another caring for them so.

I had been alone,
for so long
had felt alone
in my loving.
Then he came,
and shared with me
the joys of the children,
their pains
and the lessons they offered.

When he wooed me,
offering his love,
my heart felt, at last,
that I had found
a home, and,
together
we would open wide the doors
and invite the children in.

He offered me
the greatest gift he could,
his trust, trust in my love.
From a man
whom life had failed,
again and again,
I valued this gift,
was honoured by this gift,
valued it even higher than his love.
As he unfolded his story
my heart ached, deep and painful aching,
taking in each tale
and holding it safe.
I thought, at times,
that it could hold no more,
like a dam
trying to contain the ocean,
and it ached within my breast.

Yet, this man
was so much in need
of loving,
and gave so much to me,
gave me his trust.

He was more in need
even than the gypsy children,
and so I loved.

It seemed to me that,
wrapped in our loving,
he felt the dawning
of forgiveness,
a growing recognition
that in his life
he had been torn,
and crushed
by the cruel arms
of angry spirits,
not for what he had caused
but as a sacrifice
proffered for the sins
of others.

In those early days
of our loving,
the nations
re-commenced their warring games
and he marched again, but
this time, he marched for peace
wearing no uniform,

When he climbed the podium
and spoke to a hushed crowd,
denouncing the futility of war,
speaking with the authority
of one who had learned thus
through bitter experience,
when he made the call for peace,
my spirit leapt in dance,
and I thought,
"There is healing
in this, for my lover."

Oh, how strongly we loved!
How proudly!
Loved each other, and
loved the gypsy children
whom we called
into our welcoming arms.

I grew accustomed
to the ache in my breast,
the price of loving
a man such as he,
grew even to welcome it,
but in giving
so much of my heart
to him,

sometimes, just sometimes,
I found myself
closing the doors
to my friends,
my family,
my gypsy children,
my God.

For this, I was unforgiven.

I **watched him grow stronger**
and prouder
and closed my ears
to the whispering spirits
who sought to taint
his pure countenance
with lies,
and doubts,
and angry recriminations.

I knew him best,
I was his chosen.
He had given to me
the most precious gift
of his trust,
and I would stand by him,
whatever the cost
to my soul,
I would never be a one
to betray his trust in me.
I was proud,
honoured,
afraid.

The whispering spirits
took possession
of the weak and insecure
who coveted
the love and loyalty
the gypsy children
gave so freely to us.

Screaming, banshee cries
followed us,
haunted us,
drove us away
from the children.

Still, my home
was with him
and I followed, always,
unquestioningly.
If all I had
in this pitiful existence
was my place
beside him,
I would be happy.

For this, I was unforgiven.

Foolish,
my life became his,
drawing my essence,
filling his own cavernous soul
with the smell of roses
and the dance of the ballet.

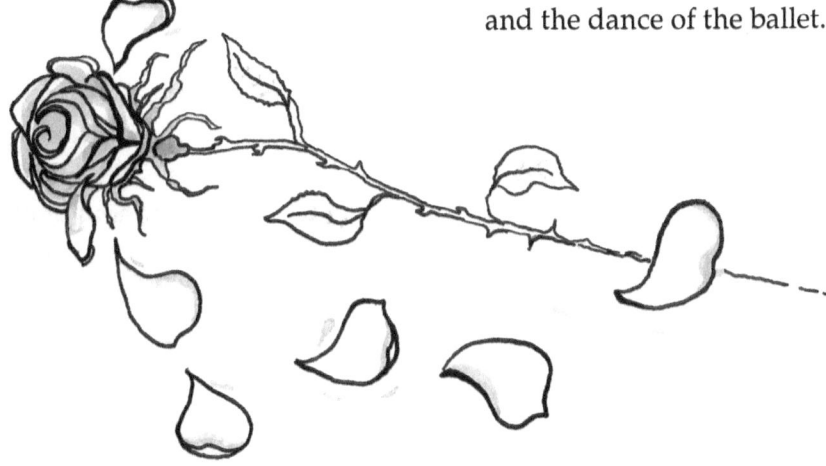

I gave it all,
gave him cool jade
to ease the fires of Hades,
but roses cannot survive
in a place devoid of light
and the ballet cannot continue
without the music.
It all faded and,
when I had no life
left to offer,
he turned me away
into the cold night
and a merciless world.

Still, I knew that with me
he had discovered
the existence
of faithful loving
that allows
the giving of trust.

He had also discovered
the fountain of perpetual youth
and when I watched
as he sought others
to restore the smell of roses,
the dam walls burst.

In the emptiness,
the emptiness of a heart
that had once held so much,
I felt still, even then,
the solid ache that was my loving,
found scattered in the ruins.

I wished him well,
wished still
that he would again
find the true loving,
such as he deserved.

I saw my wrong,
for the self is sacred
and can never be given over
to take another's
sacrificial place,
each of us
must carry our own cross
on the path to redemption.
Yet there is no great sin
in seeking, through love,
to ease another's burden.

I was forgiven,
and the light shone
again upon my world.

*A*s the light dawned,
I heard again
the insidious sighing
of the whispering spirits
and the sound
brought an eerie chill
to my already wounded heart.

No longer his chosen,
but still, I knew him best,
and none, none,
especially insubstantial whispers,
could take that from me.

The light grew ever-stronger,
the truth, more evident
as I watched him
building a new life,
and knew I watched
a stranger.
Still, I turned my eyes away
and closed my ears
so as to remain
faithful to my loving.

Louder the whispers grew,
ever more shrill
and insistent,
and once again,
I heard the banshee cry,
harsh, frightening,
signalling the death
of all we had shared,
my love and I.

I listened
to the deathly wail,
hearing deep within it
a voice so cool and clear,
a voice that had never
told me falsely,
a voice that I knew better
than any other.
Within the banshee wail,
I heard the voice
of my mother.

"You know he lied," she said,
and my world shattered.
The facts laid out,
unquestionable, concrete facts,
and how I hated them.

His story,
the story with which
he so honoured me,
the story with which
he gained such accolade,
the story was false!
Lying to the woman,
Lying to the gypsy children,
Lying to his self.

So much that was precious,
rendered untrue, worthless,
the pain absorbed,
the pain with which he purchased
my very essence,
false!
My giving, without purpose.

Never the man of this story,
though he knew the games well,
and played us all,
that was true enough!
A thief of stories,
he told tales of pain and loneliness,
of abuse and abandonment,
of war of blood-letting of torture,
he told these stories that were not his
for the honour it accorded him,
for the sympathy it gained,
for the excuses we made
for his broken soul
that we sought then to repair.
He played upon
our lesser intelligence
(as it appeared to him),
he preyed upon our bleeding hearts.

Sought the accolades of gypsy children
awed by one who had survived war,
who had killed and been tortured,
and they who knew it was not safe to trust
learned to trust him, to believe in someone.

Wearing medals
earned by others,
he had never even visited
the country where so many found
the road to Calvary.

A scuttling crab
dressed in lion's garb
that he found lying
amongst the driftwood
that lined the beach!

Now, now he is returned
to his beginning times,
a night, a dark night of the soul,
when the winds blow chill,
when even the moon
hides her light from mortal eyes.

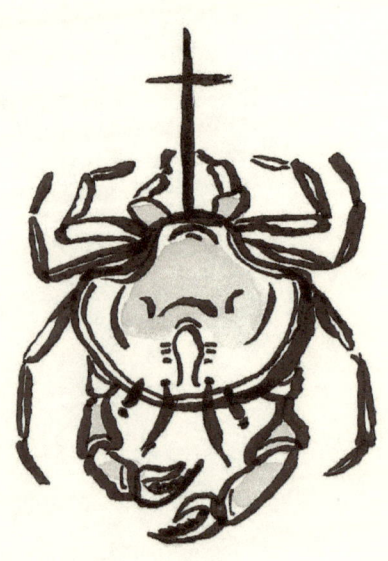

He has for too long
escaped his crucifixion.
For the lies he told
to the gypsy children that trusted him,
to the woman that loved him,
for using the pain of others
to buy his kingly robes,
for the sins we know
and those we do not,
for all of this he shall be
nailed to the cross,
displayed upon the top of the mount
where all can point and laugh
and mock his penitence
as he mocked others.
We know him now
for who he is beneath the robes,
we know him to be
the Unforgiven.